Basement Beauty

by Carmilla Voiez

Cover art by: Nicola Ormerod
Edited by: Vanessa Knipe
Poetry for Basement Beauty written by: Glen W Hunter.

This is a work of fiction. All of the characters, organizations and events portrayed in this novel are a product of the author's imagination. Any resemblance to persons, living or dead, actual events, or organizations is entirely coincidental.

Other work by Carmilla Voiez

Novels

The Ballerina and the Revolutionary

The Starblood Series -

Book 1 – Starblood

Book 2 – Psychonaut

Book 3 – Black Sun

Book 4 – Ribbons

Book 5 – Pariah

The Venus Virus

Graphic Novels

Starblood , with art by Anna Prashkovich

Psychonaut, with art by Anna Prashkovich

Short Stories

Broken Mirror and Other Morbid Tales

The Erotic Tales of Carmilla Voiez

Find out more at - www.carmillavoiez.com

~ 1 ~

'You're too beautiful to be killed, Tay,' Lynsey assured her, brushing a manicured hand through freshly lightened hair.

'What the fuck do you mean?' Amalthea shook her head, jostling afro curls and revealing a petulant frown that drew her plump cheeks inwards.

'Aint you heard? All the victims were ugly. Aint gonna happen to you, kiddo.'

Amalthea gazed at the empty pint glass in her hands. 'Ugly?'

'Yeah, not grotesque freaks or anything, just plain ugly: big noses, crooked teeth, greasy hair, you know. When I went to the dentist this morning they told me everyone and their f'in dog's booked in for cosmetic work.'

'Isn't that odd?' Amalthea rotated the glass between caramel fingers.

Lynsey shrugged. 'Dunno.'

'I think it's odd.'

'Whatever, girl. Just stop stressing, okay? You're too beautiful to die.'

Amalthea glanced over the bar at the almost empty space. 'Seems quiet tonight.'

'Yeah, well it's still early. Heard there's a gig on. Lots of people probably there. They'll lurch in here eventually.' Lynsey wiped down the counter with a damp cloth.

'Hope so. Drags when it's this quiet.' Amalthea placed the clean glass on a shelf at knee level. 'Makes me want to open a book.'

Lynsey nodded. 'Why don't you? Mind if I pop out for a ciggie?'

Amalthea nodded toward the dimly lit room and grimaced. 'Uh yeah. I think I can manage these three alone.'

'Cheers, babes.' Lynsey kissed Amalthea's cheek and exited through a door between rows of optics.

Amalthea dried another glass from the crate and set it on the shelf. She repeated the action until the crate was empty without being disturbed by customers. When she looked up again she noticed a young man, strolling towards her. She recognised him from poetry nights. As always, he arrived alone. This evening he carried a slender book. She tried to see the cover, but it was angled away from her.

'Hi,' she said as he sat on a stool.

He smiled warmly. He was pretty, for a white boy. His skin seemed to have the soft glow of health that was rare in young men from this Scottish city. He reminded Amalthea of the father she hadn't seen in over a decade, except this lad was even paler and his eyes resembled emeralds held in front of a flame.

'Coffee, please.'

Amalthea nodded. She had never known him to order alcohol. Most of the patrons were ardent drinkers and this boy… man stood out for his lack of inebriation. Was he too young to drink or a recovering alcoholic? Maybe he found other ways to relax: the words clutched in his hand or ones in his head. He fascinated her, although she wasn't sure why. Physically, sexually, he wasn't her type, but there was something about his gentle calm that attracted her and what better time to strike up a conversation than a quiet night like this?

She switched on the coffee machine and poured in freshly ground beans.

'Seems quiet,' he said.

'Very,' she answered. 'What brings you here tonight? I normally just see you on poetry nights.'

'You notice?' he asked and his eyes gleamed brighter.

Not another one? The club attracted would-be creeps and admirers. It was hard to tell the difference between the two from the other side of the bar. She hastily backtracked. 'Sure. I know all my regulars. Do you write poetry?'

'I'm not sure it's any good.'

'Ahhh, you should perform a piece one night. It's a friendly crowd. They won't bite.'

He laughed. 'Yeah, maybe. It could be fun… Do you write?'

'Prose,' she answered. 'Nothing published. What book is that?'

'Plath.' He flashed the cover at her.

'You like Sylvia Plath?'

'I guess I have a thing for desperate sorrow.' His face flushed and he appeared vulnerable.

She nodded, warming to him again. 'There's a lot of that in this town.'

'I'm Daniel.' He extended his exquisitely manicured right hand.

Her hand met his half way across the bar. Her chewed fingernails, chipped purple polish and brown skin made an interesting contrast. He seemed different yet the same. It confused her. 'Amalthea,' she said. 'Or Tay.'

'Delighted to make your acquaintance, Amalthea. Do you work here every night?'

'Almost.'

The machine's noise altered as coffee dripped into a mug. She passed Daniel a black coffee with no sugar – his usual order.

'Thank you.' He nodded and took a sip. 'And what do you do when you aren't here?'

'Sleep, write, oh and I'm studying English at the Uni.'

'Busy…' He seemed pensive, teetering on the edge of saying something. Whatever it was, he decided not to ask. Instead he stood up. 'Thank you, Taya.' He sauntered to a leather chair below a green spotlight.

Lynsey bustled back through the door, dragging cold air and the stench of tobacco with her. 'Did I miss anything?'

'Not much. I put the glasses away and we have a new customer.'

Lynsey stared across at Daniel and exhaled. 'Seen him before, a bit of an odd ball, quiet, always alone.'

Amalthea nodded. 'Maybe that's the way he likes it.'

~ 2 ~

Amalthea stood outside the unlit staff-entrance to The Pit and breathed in the cool, pre-dawn air. One hand brushed wild curls from her mouth and tucked them behind her ear. They sprang back across her cheek immediately, untameable.

As her skin acclimatised she drew jacket sleeves over her arms. A movement at the edge of her vision attracted her attention and she peered towards the shadowy alley where the bins were stored. Her direct gaze didn't reveal any ghoul, goblin, animal or person skulking in the darkness, watching and waiting for her to leave, but her mind created a sinister shape.

For the past six weeks the evening news had continually reported unnatural deaths city-wide. Rumours of a modern day Jack the Ripper were rife. Now every alleyway had become hostile territory and every shadow a killer, preparing to strike.

Amalthea buttoned her coat. Home wasn't far away, a mere ten minute walk. By four in the morning most of the drunks were already home, sleeping it off, or standing, unsteadily in taxi queues, waiting for chariots to return them safely to their beds. That was one thing to be said about fear of what might lurk the dark – it was good for the economy.

Gentle but pervasive drizzle vainly attempted to flatten her hair. Street lights mutated into dancing constellations, and pavements were dotted with quicksilver puddles. Amalthea's boots leaked, and the liquid made her toes squelch. Sucking and dripping sounds masked the noise of her footsteps and the perfectly matched slapping of shoe leather behind. Of course, the street was empty when she glanced back, but the moment she faced forwards she felt a presence behind her, matching her stride. The shadow from which she fled, unseen but perceived through all her other senses, making her hairline tingle – the man who wasn't there.

She'd tried to tell Lynsey of this consuming fear, but her friend hadn't understood, dismissing it as paranoia. She decided in the future to only mention this deep, primal knowledge to her diary and wondered for one terrifying moment whether his other victims had known they were being hunted, but had kept silent or were disbelieved until the moment their vacated shells were discovered.

Her scalp itched. Realising the utter pointlessness of another backwards glance, she balled her fists and marched onwards. In five more minutes she could lock the darkness outside, for what that was worth.

A shriek broke through the pittering-pattering shroud of raindrops. It echoed between tall Victorian town houses, converted into flats and bedsits – a cat or a baby waking from a nightmare? She waited for a repeat of the noise until she became aware that she was standing, still as a statue, while the rain continued to fall around and upon her. The sound didn't return. Shivering, she willed her right foot to take a step forward, asked her hip to tilt and her knee to bend. Movement didn't follow her commands so she concentrated on her left foot instead – still nothing. Swallowing hard, she wiggled the toes of her left foot. Water moved between skin and cotton; the sensation made her nauseous.

'Just walk, Tay,' she whispered.

Rain hissed in her ears, and a waterfall tumbled from her chin onto her chest.

'Just walk… five minutes!'

A tree shook water from its leaves like a huge dog. Large drops splattered as they hit the ground. What waited beyond that tree, hidden behind the trunk? She considered taking a longer route home where the streets were less shadowy and the traffic more regular.

Shivering from cold and fear, she watched the heavy branches bend and purge until the urge to vomit returned.

How many had been killed already this year? Ten, no twelve – would she be the thirteenth? She shook her head; this fear was not rational. She wasn't being hunted and her home was a mere five minute walk from this spot. Five minutes – she could walk for five minutes. Five minutes – no distance at all yet one step forwards felt beyond her reach.

'Tay, get a grip!' Her mind used her mother's voice – dominant, matriarchal and full of a rich, musical patois. She nodded, fighting her foolishness and the paralysing fear of what – a tree, a shadow, a lone shriek? What set her off this time? 'You is fierce, a powerful woman. This shit is beneath you, Amalthea. You shame me.'

Raising her head, she blinked diamonds from her eyes. The raindrops altered their route and formed puddles within the cradles of her earlobes. With Herculean effort, she stepped forward. Once freed from their trap her legs adopted a natural rhythm. Swift and sure she passed beneath the branches as a single sphere fell and trickled between her neck and jacket collar. In less than five minutes she reached home, pushing bolts into place and turning keys in locks.

The breath she took filled her lungs with warm, dry air. She gulped it down as though it was her first breath then headed for the bathroom and a towel.

~ 3 ~

'I heard there was another one last night,' Lynsey said.

They stood together behind the bar, scanning the room. Another night another dollar.

'Another murder?' Amalthea asked. 'Does that make it thirteen now?'

'Yes and they still don't have a clue who's doing it. Is my make up okay? How about my hair? I could do with going to the stylist again, but it's so expensive.'

'You look fine.'

'I wonder whether they all thought that? And I know I could do with losing a few pounds. Oh stop sneering, Amalthea. The latest victim is another woman. That's eight women and five men. Do you think he prefers women? Do you think the men were accidents? The last five have all been women, right?'

Amalthea shrugged. 'I don't know, Lynsey.'

'Don't walk home alone tonight. Promise me,' Lynsey said.

'I thought you said I was too beautiful to die.'

'Just in case. People are talking about setting up vigilante groups. It's going to get really bad. I can feel it in my stomach.'

Amalthea shook her head. 'I can't afford a taxi and I've got no one to walk with.'

'How about if I stay back, tonight? Give you a lift home.'

'What about your kids?'

'I can be late for one night,' Lynsey assured her.

'What about tomorrow and the next night and the night after that?'

'Maybe they'll catch him.'

'You think?'

'No, but each day at a time, right? Stay alive today and let tomorrow take care of itself.'

'Seems pointless,' Amalthea muttered.

'Isn't everything when you analyse it. Come on. For me. Let me drive you home.'

'Honestly, Lynsey, there's no need.'

Lynsey patted Amalthea's arm. 'I don't want to walk to the car park alone.'

Amalthea exhaled loudly then nodded. 'Sure. It'd be great if you dropped me home tonight. I'd feel much safer.'

'Thanks, babes. I wonder if it'll be busy tonight. Do you think they'll set a curfew?'

'What? The police? Shit, I hope not. I'll be screwed. How will I pay rent?'

'Well, it's only eight o'clock. I guess it's too early to panic about the emptiness. Wish we had something on tonight though. Something to attract the punters away from their TV sets and out into the frosty night.' Lynsey chewed a nail then stopped and stared at her fingers. She rubbed the slightly chipped polish, frowning. 'Dammit.'

At the end of the quiet night, the tills were emptied and the safe filled. Amalthea locked the back door behind them. Lynsey interlocked her arm with Amalthea's. 'Your carriage awaits, Ma'am.'

They hurried towards the car park as rain fell from the starless sky. Mist obscured the street lights and the air was chill. The Mini with its super heating system beckoned them, and they rushed towards it arm in arm.

Only one other car remained in the car park. It was at the far side, at least twenty metres away from them and it appeared empty.

The two friends almost fell through the doors into the low seats.

'Mmmmm,' Lynsey said.

Amalthea nodded. 'Thanks for the lift.'

'Thanks for walking me to the car.'

'No problem at all,' Amalthea replied.

Lynsey switched on the lights, put the car into gear and drove away. Neither of them noticed that the lights of the other car switched on or that a large, dark vehicle followed them out of the compound.

~ 4 ~

'This was left for you,' Gareth said, handing Amalthea an envelope the moment she arrived at The Pit for her shift.

'Who's it from?' she asked.

'Fecked if I know. Open it and find out.'

'Did you see who left it?'

'No it was stuffed through the letter box this morning.'

Amalthea studied the sealed envelope then wandered off.

'Not going to share the secret with me, then?' Gareth asked.

'Not this time,' she answered.

'Oh, Lynsey phoned. Kid's sick. I'd stay but I have a thing later. Will you be okay?'

'Who else is coming in?' Amalthea called over her shoulder.

'Jamie and Steve at ten.'

'Friday. Band night. Might be a bit tight. What time are you leaving?'

'Not until eleven.'

'Jamie and Steve staying til the end?'

'Yup.'

'We'll manage. You do your thing.'

'Awesome! Don't stress about tidying the place. The cleaners are in tomorrow morning. Just cash up and get your ass home.'

'Will do.' Amalthea tore open the envelope. Inside was a scribbled note.

Amalthea, you enchant me. I want to know what hides behind your smile. You are everything that is good in this world and you deserve the purest love imaginable. Meet me when your shift ends and I will gladly show you what you mean to me. Eternally yours, Daniel.

'What is it?' Gareth asked.

'Nothing,' Amalthea answered, folding the paper into a cube and stuffing it into her jeans pocket.

Amalthea was too busy behind the bar to say goodbye to her boss when he left. Luckily Jamie and

Steve worked hard and no customer was ignored. The music was mellow indie rock – not Amalthea's taste, but pleasant enough. At least it wasn't ear-splitting punk. Some Fridays she wished she could wear ear-plugs. Having to walk home in the middle of the night, ears ringing in a tone she would never hear again, wasn't her idea of a good time.

She dried a hot pint glass and popped it onto the rack to cool. 'I'd better collect glasses,' Amalthea said, tapping Jamie on the shoulder.

Jamie nodded. 'Hurry back.'

Amalthea weaved between bodies. The club was full of grungy student types with dirty jeans and oily hair. Many of the men were unshaven, rough stubble not beards, threatening to scratch anyone who dared get too close. They reminded Amalthea of cacti. She returned to the bar red-faced and breathless, but without breaking a single glass.

'Glad you're back. Could do with a hand,' Jamie said.

'Where's Steve?'

'The band needed help with the sound system.'

The patrons grumbled. They did not like to wait for their alcoholic refreshments. Amalthea shifted up a gear and cleared the queue before Steve returned.

~ 5 ~

Daniel stroked the thick, dark hair of a woman as she nestled her face in his lap. Her flesh was covered in goose bumps. He cupped her chin and tilted her head until her glassy eyes stared blankly in the general direction of his face. He searched for her once wild spirit, crouching somewhere behind that expressionless face.

Her neck was bruised purple and green. Red juice, from the strawberries he fed her, dripped down her chin. He smudged it around her mouth with his thumb, licking his lips as the heat of his desire rose. She didn't react to the change in his body, his hardness. He tugged her hair until she yelped. As her body relaxed the dull thud of metal against stone resonated through the cellar. She peered up at him and the chain rose with her, the chain he had attached to the metal collar around her throat.

He remembered when he met Emily; she'd been dancing – magnificent in her graceful movements, fiercely exciting, playful and intelligent. Qualities she'd long since buried.

Amalthea's face filled his thoughts. Perhaps she was the one. Could she love him as an equal?

'Would you like a new playmate?' he asked.

Emily's eyes darkened. Anger or jealousy? He wasn't sure which.

'Tell me what you want, Emily.'

'I want to go home.' Her voice was a hoarse whisper. 'Please, let me go home.'

'You know I can't do that, Emily.'

'Then kill me, drain me. I can't – don't make me. Set me free, please.'

'I won't drink from you, Emily.'

'Why? I know what you are, what you do – I know what you want.'

Daniel shook his head. 'You're wrong. That isn't what I want.'

'But I've seen you.'

He stroked her hair. 'I won't ever hurt you, Emily. I promise.'

She shuddered under his caresses. 'Why am I here? What do you want from me?'

'I love you.'

She spat at him. 'You call this love?'

Daniel's hand moved and Emily crawled into the shadows as far away from him as her chain would allow. He knelt beside her and stroked her cheek. She shuddered again. Fear drained from her eyes and became empty voids. She was never there when he kissed her or touched her with a tenderness he was certain she would enjoy if she allowed herself. He held his arms open for her. 'At least let me warm you.'

She nodded and moved closer. 'You could give me clothes,' she whispered.

His arms encircled her cold, damp body – fragile in his arms. She was losing too much weight. 'You should eat more. Don't you like the food I give you?'

She didn't answer. Her cheek rested against his chest, where his heartbeat might have been if he was human.

'I do love you,' he told her, stroking and untangling her hair. 'I wish you could see that.'

Her body felt limp against his and he realised she had fallen asleep. He stood up, cradling her in his arms like a baby. A soft mattress with angora blankets and silk sheets butted up against whitewashed stones. He laid her on it and reclined beside her, one hand supporting his cheek and the other resting on her tiny waist. He kissed her brow and pulled the luxurious covers over her flesh then arranged the chain so she was unlikely to entangle herself if she moved in her sleep.

When Emily and he were first courting, their conversations had stimulated him beyond all measure. How could loving a mind as fine as hers be wrong? After years of psychoanalysis, he still couldn't see a beautiful human face without wanting to kiss it. Their body parts fitted perfectly and while they were unable to procreate it was insane to believe that sex was merely a tool for making babies. If he could explain it to the others – but that was impossible when every relationship with a human ended like this – a chained, half-starved body in the basement. Potential never fulfilled, love never returned, the flame of desire extinguished before it had time to light the shadows of his soul. His love for them damned him and he knew that as well as anyone. He couldn't change what he wanted; he only wished it was possible to keep their love after they discovered his nature. Amalthea would be different. She was strong, exciting, dominant and confident. She might be the one person in the whole filthy world able to heal him, change him and help him to show his family why a human was worthy of love.

He would recite poetry for Amalthea. Human women fell in love so easily with language. The right words whispered in an ear sent shivers of pleasure across flesh. How in touch with their longing humans were. Perhaps that was why their lives were so short. If they lived for hundreds of years, their impact on the world and each other would be immeasurable. The thought excited him, taboo though it was.

Vampires had achieved so little of note over the millennia that their history books were mere pamphlets. Where were the DaVincis and the Shakespeares of his species? Longevity was a curse, delaying every action for want of any sense of urgency. There was no need to create something to outlive you when you expected to live forever. Only science attracted the minds of vampires, mostly in order to perfect a vampire master race and eradicate heterogeneity. Perhaps, more than longevity that was the curse of the vampires – that they were all expected to think alike and act alike. Art could never thrive in such a stifling environment.

Leaving Emily to her dreams, he returned upstairs and pulled out a photograph and a pad of writing paper from the desk in his study. The picture was of Amalthea, standing outside the door to The Pit, eyes half closed, completely at peace with herself. He envied her stillness and the way she seemed complete within her own skin. She was magnificent.

He picked up a pen and allowed the nib to hover just above the paper. *What should I write?* It needed to be personal, from the heart. It needed to resonate within her as something she would wish to say to a lover and yearn to hear.

Amalthea, you enchant me. I want to know what hides behind your smile. You are everything that is good in this world and you deserve the purest love imaginable. Meet me when your shift ends and I will gladly show you what you mean to me. Eternally yours, Daniel.

He folded the letter into a rich plum-coloured envelope, scribed her name upon it then drove to the city to stuff it through the letterbox of the club before he could change his mind.

He drove back to his house, thinking about Amalthea and all the loves he'd had before, the women he'd pursued and captured only to watch them shrivel and become less human. Was it like collecting butterflies, destroying life by trying to pin it in place?

Humans were not like vampires. Their feelings were complex and tainted by fear of their mortality. They entered wholeheartedly into love affairs; it was their way of staying ahead of death. In contrast vampire love seemed transitory and hollow, meaningless. Simply a source of physical pleasure and occasionally procreation, not the life affirming, spiritual ecstasy he witnessed among humans lucky enough to find someone they loved.

If his pets had failed to deliver on this unspoken promise, perhaps it was because sex with him brought death a step closer rather than pushing it away; maybe they knew this instinctively and maybe Amalthea would too. He hoped not, but prepared himself for yet another disappointment.

It had taken years to understand that these women, who seemed so loving at first, might choose to betray him and leave. That he kept them imprisoned was their fault not his. He wanted to share his house with them, tuck each one into bed at night. If only they understood that he wasn't a threat to them, but they were blind to his love and devotion – heartless and careless of his desires. It made him sad, but it was better than living alone.

He prepared dinner, filled four glasses with wine and took it all to the cellar. A bare light bulb made the space appear bright and soulless. He placed a plate and glass in front of Emily. Grunting, she sat up. Moving further into the maze of rooms and corridors, he took food and wine to the other women.

Diane had been a waitress in a coffee shop where he used to hang out and watch hipsters drink lattes and plan their lives. He offered to walk her home one evening when her shift ended. Her smile was warm and intelligent, but she didn't smile for him now. She hardly moved when he placed her dinner in front of her mattress. He stroked her hair, trying to wake her, but she seemed deep in some dream. He hoped it was a good one.

Charlie had been an exotic dancer. He'd seen a poster featuring her outside a strip club in Soho. She had lived with him for two years and her once plump figure had all but vanished over that time. Her arms now defined by narrow bones.

'Please eat,' he whispered as he placed his offering before her. Her green eyes flickered open, but there was no trace of recognition in her stare. He touched her hair and moved on.

Finally he reached Moira, remembering how he met her in a library. She had so many books that she hardly had the strength to carry them to her car. He helped her, then watched the library for three weeks until she returned. It was Moira who had first sparked his interest in poetry. She loved the romance of language and the more expert he became in its use the more she fell in love with him. The first time they made love she cried. She said he was beautiful and made him believe it. They lived happily together for three months until she found the key to his cellar. In the end he had to slap her when hysteria threatened to choke her. She fell to the floor, hitting her head on the edge of a table and from that moment she hadn't spoken a word to him. He no longer felt beautiful when she looked at him. Now he felt like a monster. He blindfolded her so he no longer saw his reflection in her pale blue eyes. When he left her food he placed a spoon within her palm and directed her hand to the plate. She never removed the cloth from her eyes. Perhaps she was more comfortable in the dark or perhaps seeing him was too terrible for her to bear.

He'd had other pets before these. In one week he lost an entire batch to flu. He'd mopped their brows and fed them penicillin, but they never recovered their appetites even when their fevers broke. Heartbroken, he vowed never to take another woman home, but six weeks later he was hunting again, searching for another pretty face and clever mind with whom to spend his evenings. It was an addiction, but there were no self-help groups for people like him.

He wandered back through the cellar, past Charlie who was ignoring the platter completely in favour of some dream and past Diane who had woken and was playing listlessly with her food. As he reached the corner, he slipped and barely recovered his footing. He clung to the wall for support. Wet, warm and sticky, it coated his skin in delicious, sensual ways. Everything was red. He feared sickness; if he forgot to feed for too long, a crimson mania took over. He touched his forehead, but his fingers slid against the skin as if oiled. Red spread out below his feet, seeping across the room. The wall was dotted with it. He recognised the smell and, like any great connoisseur, knew the vintage. He sucked the tip of his index finger – a ripe, earthy jus with tangy head notes of iron – Emily's blood.

He followed the trail to a slumped body and gathered her in his arms. Glass shards glinted in an ocean of blood. Her wrists and throat had been sliced and her heartbeat silenced, but on her face was a smile that chilled him more than the vision of her splattered blood. It was a smile of relief, pleased to be free at last. He held her closer and wept.

While he mourned, he cleaned her flesh with his tongue and saw himself as she had always seen him – a monster.

~ 6 ~

He cleaned his skin and changed his clothes before returning to Diane's cell. She was still asleep and hadn't touched her food, so he left it there for her. Moira was finishing her meal.

'Hello Moira.'

She lifted her head.

'I've written a new poem. Would you like to hear it?'

She nodded.

'I gave her my heart after years of promises
and she ran screaming from the room as it
pulsed in my hand
I couldn't understand why it didn't go as
planned
Maybe my love was too literal
Visceral and exposed like a raw nerve
Too quick to serve myself to her this way

I've always been too impulsive

Quick to follow my sorrow down the wrong

street

The sound of feet

Running

Charging

Headlong into memories lane down a soon

forgotten path

A run-down, ransacked and rancid math

of you subtracted from me

equalling   nothing   but   fractions   and

remainders

but these are the dangers of Cupid's bow

Love will come

Love will grow

Love will go

or wither on the vine

In this green house of time there are many

dead roses.'

The words trickled into her consciousness and he saw pleasure in her face. When he finished he kissed her dry lips.

'I miss you,' he told her. He stroked her blindfold and she quivered slightly. 'Shall I take this off?'

She shook her head, defiantly. 'I cannot look at you.' The words sounded cracked and broken, like her lips. They chilled him.

'Why?' he asked.

'Because the fire of my hatred will consume us both,' Moira replied.

He hung his head and blinked away tears. 'I'm sorry.'

'Not sorry enough,' she rasped.

He sat beside her in silence.

'I can smell blood on you,' she said.

He took Charlie's and Moira's empty dishes with him as he climbed the stairs, knowing the only impact his removal from this world would have on anyone was a sense of relief. Even Charlie, Moira and Diane, although they would probably starve, would see his absence as a blessing – a chance to fade into dust.

It wasn't fair. He was a better man than most of his kind. He beautified his victims, gave them a luminescence and mystery in death that they lacked in life. He killed the most clumsy, the most ugly humans he found then made them precious, creating statues of their cold flesh. It was his gift to humanity, and part of him wanted to be acknowledged, appreciated for his art, by humans and other vampires.

He wandered restlessly through empty rooms, sleep eluding his grasp, his body and mind agitated. Hiding his nature, behind sickening cowardice, had become a chain around his neck, trapping him like the women in his cellar.

Would tonight change anything? Meeting Amalthea outside The Pit, he would be tempted to throw himself – body and soul – at her, but such actions although acceptable among his own kind tended to frighten human females. More subtlety was required. He found himself, mentally debating every choice, every move before he made it. Perhaps by desiring humans he was simply exchanging one set of rules that had been etched onto his skin by centuries of training, for others that were alien and confusing. That was what frustrated him most, his lifestyle was not the easy choice; it was hard and full of challenges from every direction. What fool could think he would ever choose to be this way or could be taught to be something different?

He hovered in the hallway, clutching his car keys, shoulders hunched and raised almost to the bottom of his earlobes, hands in fists, and knees locked. A thousand voices rushed around his mind advising different courses of action. He wanted to drown them out but they persisted. Unable to stand this stasis any longer, he fled the house, started his car and headed towards Glasgow and Amalthea.

~ 7 ~

'Hi, Taya,' Daniel said as she reached the corner.

Amalthea jumped.

'I'm sorry,' he said. 'I've scared you. Did you get my letter?'

She nodded, clenching her jaw. She suspected that she must have appeared comical, but Daniel didn't laugh.

'You're in danger,' he told her.

She shook her head. 'I won't let you hurt me,' she growled.

'Not from me.' He stretched his palms towards her and knelt on the wet pavement in supplication. 'I don't want to hurt you.'

She glared at him, silently. *Fuck you! Get out of my life!* If she could have strangled him with a look alone he would have already fallen to the floor.

'You make me want to be a better person.'

Her throat tightened and her skin crawled.

He stood up and extended his slender fingers towards her face. Something pinched her hard. Her legs gave way as she swooned.

Her throat quivered on the edge of a scream. Head throbbing, she was disorientated, lost, stupid. This was a nightmare, a dream; any moment she would wake up and it would all be over. He carried her, cradling her head and behind her knees. Then she felt herself sink into a car seat and still her voice failed her.

The car headed out of the city. Even if her brain had been working properly, they were travelling too fast to risk jumping from the vehicle; perhaps, she hoped, she could escape when they stopped at traffic lights. Daniel's voice sounded crystal clear through the car speakers. The damned stereo was reciting his poetry.

What do I have to offer you, but poetry and
true love?
An infinite heart that never beats
A face scarred by too many ages
Pages of my life which curl at the corners
Previous bookmarks left by long lost lovers

My cover pristine in a moon light dream that
will never end
The clock's hands warp and bend
Coiling into a figure eight fallen on its side
Endless empty rooms of dead potential
Just graves above ground without corpses
Sources of solitude and sorrow
There is no tomorrow
Only the infinity of the moment
and a past always far too present for
comfort.

The recorded voice was hypnotic. Yawning, she realised how tired she felt and how hot the car was.

Sweet and sure sanctuary surrounds your
soul
Soothing and warm,
shelter from the storm.
Slipping into the perfect circles of your eyes,
I fall head first with only the broken compass
of my heart as a guide

I feel you inside
Under pale and worn flesh
Quickening this dead thing
I can hear your soul sing
In a minor key of being free whilst playing
with your locks...

Amalthea woke in a strange bed. The room was oppressively dark. Letting her eyes adjust, she realised that a sliver of sunlight framed two parallel rectangles on the wall opposite her bed. Staring harder, she saw shutters and wandered over to open them.

The room filled with light. Through the window she saw a large lawn studded with trees and hemmed in by an ancient stone wall. She pushed open the sash and leaned outside. The drop was no more than twelve feet, but there was nothing to use to climb out and pavingstones waited directly below. If she jumped, she would break a bone or two.

She heard the click of a lock and spun around, feeling inexplicably guilty. The door opened and Daniel stepped into the room. He screwed up his eyes against the brightness of the light.

'You're awake,' he said. 'Would you like breakfast in here or will you join me in the kitchen?'

Amalthea took a step forward. 'Is there coffee?'

'Yes.'

Amalthea followed him into a showroom-style kitchen. Daniel's wealth screamed from every surface, from the tiled floor to the pristine Aga oven. She had never felt so out of place in her life. Watching him carefully, she took of sip from her cup.

'We have eggs, bacon, sausages, croissants, jam, cake, fruit and toast. Do you prefer orange, grapefruit or apple juice?' he asked.

'No meat,' she said. 'Anything else is fine.'

'Coming up.' He placed a plate loaded with sweet pastries and a glass of what appeared to be freshly squeezed juice on the table then sat opposite her, watching.

'What are you going to eat?' Amalthea stared at him then glanced at her own full plate.

'I woke a couple of hours ago. I already had breakfast.'

'Can I have more coffee please?' she asked, standing up.

'Let me,' he replied, taking her cup to the opposite end of the kitchen where a full coffee jug was being kept warm.

He returned with two mugs and passed hers across the table, placing it beside her juice. Her muddled thoughts fell into place; she saw a large window over a Belfast sink surrounded by empty work surfaces. To the left of the window was a glass paned door that stood slightly ajar. Knowing that she was not locked in made her feel slightly better, but she had already seen the large garden and the trees beyond its stone outer walls and knew there was not a road or any other house in sight. How isolated was this place? The open door might simply be a ploy to manipulate her into feeling less trapped.

'Where are we?' she asked.

'In the kitchen... of my home... in Scotland.'

'Where in Scotland?' Amalthea asked.

'A little north of Perth,' he answered.

She nodded. 'How far away is the nearest town or village?'

He shrugged. 'A couple of miles, I guess.'

'Do I get a guided tour of your home?'

'I'll show you around. Have you finished?'

She nodded although the pastries remained untouched.

'Obviously this is the kitchen. There's a double fridge that I keep well stocked. There's also a wine-rack down here – all reds. Is that okay or shall I get some white wine in for you?'

'Red's fine. What's through there?' she asked as they passed a closed wooden door with a keyhole.

'The pantry.' Daniel kept walking.

She noticed a knife block on the granite work surface and a hook with keys hanging from it by the back door. As she followed Daniel, she scanned every wall for weapons, keys and exit routes. They entered a large room with flocked wallpaper, an imposing leather three piece suite and a dominating fireplace, over which hung an intricately carved sword sheath. She remembered with a sense of doom the origins of the word vagina and shuddered. The ornate handle and elegant container suggested a samurai sword – a katana. Was it sharp?

'The living room,' he said. 'We have lots of books here, a music system and a television set. There are countless channels, but most of them seem pretty pointless, to be honest.'

They crossed the hallway again and Amalthea glanced at the front door. It was probably locked, but there were windows on either side. They entered another room with a table large enough to seat twelve people.

'The dining room,' he said.

She nodded, feeling a profound sense of hollowness. Nothing seemed real. The house was a film set, no one actually lived here. They were acting out parts – a scene in a movie. She noted a few pictures on the deep red wall, but nothing to hurt him. He walked around the table and motioned to a black object on a shelf.

'There's a music system in here too.' He sounded proud as if what he owned was the result of some great and heroic quest.

He passed her again and exited the room. They followed a narrow corridor on the right, beyond the mouth of the staircase. It led to a second living room. Amalthea imagined it would have served as a drawing room when the house was built, centuries ago. More books lined the walls and a chaise-longue crouched beneath a shuttered window. Unless her sense of direction had failed her, this window would open out over the same garden as her bedroom. The only other item in this room was a large lamp, heavy enough to do some damage.

'That's the toilet and shower room.' He pointed.

He opened the next door and Amalthea glanced inside. A wooden medicine cabinet was screwed to the only tile-free wall. There were no medicines, no razors nor toothbrushes inside.

The final door led to a cold room with a stone floor. Empty shelves covered two of the walls and another closed door hung on the final wall. On one top shelf she noticed the edge of a single wooden box.

'I think this was a workshop. The garage is through there,' he said, pointing at the second door.

He didn't open the door to the garage. Instead he led her upstairs. Stained glass windows covered the wall where the stairs veered left and continued their ascent. A few paintings of landscapes hung there and Amalthea realised that she had noticed no photographs or anything that resembled a family portrait.

'This is your room, of course.' Daniel pointed towards a door on the right. 'And this is mine.'

'Can we go in?' Amalthea asked.

'Not just now. It's a bit messy,' he replied.

'This is the main bathroom.' He opened a door to a large room with marble tiles on the walls and floors and an elegant footed bathtub. 'You are welcome to consider this your bathroom. I've got an en suite. I bought you a toothbrush and paste. If you need a different brand let me know. There's also shampoo and conditioner, bubble bath and shower gel. I don't think I forgot anything.'

'Is there a razor… for shaving my legs?'

He looked at her strangely. 'I – I'm sorry. I didn't think… I'll get one for you.'

'I won't be here long. There's no need.'

'Just in case. I want you to have everything you desire while you're here.'

'I guess you'd better get sanitary towels too then.'

He blanched.

He took her to three other doors on that level. 'I haven't done anything in these rooms yet apart from add a bed and wardrobe. Sorry if they seem a bit characterless. I don't use them.'

'What's upstairs?' she asked.

'More empty rooms. This place has twelve bedrooms. Do you want to see?'

'An attic too?'

'Sure,' he said. 'There's another set of stairs up to the attic. It's empty though.'

'Can I see?'

'Of course. Do you want to wander by yourself or shall I come with you?'

'I'm fine by myself.' She climbed the next staircase. The rooms up there were shuttered too; she opened them to let the daylight enter. The rooms were empty, but clean. In some of them second doors led to unused wardrobes and cupboards, but the hiding possibilities were limited. There were no weapons and the windows were too high to use as a means for escape unless she planned to climb onto the roof. The attic was bare except for a few spider webs. Shadows reached for her in the deathly quiet, empty space and she shivered with cold and fear then quickly left, shutting the door behind her.

~ 8 ~

She found a note from Daniel in the kitchen: *Popped out for a few minutes. Please help yourself to lunch.* She opened the refrigerator and closed it again, wondering how much time she had. What did Daniel mean when he said a few minutes?

She climbed the staircase and tried his bedroom door. It was locked so she hurried back downstairs to the workshop. The second door wasn't locked; it opened easily when she pressed the handle. It led, as he had said it would, into a garage. There was no car inside, but a number of tools on rough pine shelves that might prove useful. She tried opening the external garage door, but that was locked. Shutting the interior doors behind her, she returned to the hallway checked the front then the kitchen door and found both locked. She remembered the keys and looked for them. The larger set had gone, presumably Daniel had taken them with him, but there was a smaller set left. She pulled these off the wall and tried all the locked doors, but none of the keys fitted any of the locks. Frustrated she tried the last door, the door Daniel had told her led to the pantry. It opened with the second key, but instead of shelves laden with food or cooking utensils she saw a narrow wooden staircase leading downwards.

Nervously, she glanced over her shoulder. She heard nothing inside or outside the house and decided to risk descending. She pocketed the keys and pulled the door shut behind her. She felt her way in the dark until on the fourth step down something brushed her forehead. Clinging to the bannister with one hand, she reached up with the other, found a string and pulled it. Lights flickered on before and above her.

She followed the stairs into a cellar. At the bottom she saw a square room with a metal hoop attached to a wall and a chain arranged in a spiral on the flagstone floor. On one side was an archway. The hall beyond was lit and she heard something like whispers coming from it. Behind her she heard the sound of a car engine. Daniel must have returned. She stood still for a moment, not knowing whether to investigate further or run back up the stairs and lock the door. Softly, she called out. 'Is anyone there?'

For the briefest of moments everything was silent then Amalthea heard a rush of voices – at least three women, all talking at the same time, soft and quickly so it was impossible for her to make sense of their words. Then she heard one single voice, strong and clear. 'Help us.'

'I can hear Daniel's car. I have to go and lock the door. I'll be back as soon as I can. How many of you are there? Are you locked up?'

'Three, I think. There used to be four. We're chained to the walls. Please hurry. Help us before he comes back.'

'I can't. I don't have time, but I'll be back. I promise.'

'Hopefully before he chains you up too. Don't tell him you know about us. Keep it a secret.'

'Okay.' Amalthea's voice trembled. 'I'm sorry.'

She bolted up the stairs, locked the door, remembered that she had left on the light, unlocked the door again and switched the light off. She had locked the door and just replaced the keys on their hook when she heard Daniel's footsteps tapping along the hall from the garage and workshop. She tried to stop shaking, but found it impossible so she picked up his note, pretending to read.

He placed a carrier bag on the counter.

'Can I go out?' Amalthea asked.

He glanced over her shoulder at the window. 'It's pretty cold and damp outside, today.'

'Okay. Can I use your phone?'

'I have to charge it first,' Daniel said.

Amalthea nodded. 'Okay then. Let me know when it's charged, won't you?'

'Of course. Have you had lunch yet?' he asked.

'No.'

'What do you want?'

'Just coffee.' Amalthea's heart pounded painfully against her ribs.

'You'll waste away.'

Amalthea grimaced at his words.

'Are you okay?' he asked. His face seemed full of genuine concern and she found it impossible to reconcile the display of emotion with the voices downstairs.

Who are you? Instead of asking her question aloud, she sat down and combed her fingers through her hair, trying to stay calm.

'You're safe here,' he assured her.

'And what about my friends, my mum, my job? What about my degree?'

Daniel eyes searched her face. 'Would you like me to tell them you're okay?'

'How?' She straightened up and put her shaking hands flat against the table top.

'Drive back to Glasgow?'

'Can I come too?' Amalthea asked.

'It's probably safer if you don't,' Daniel replied.

She thought of the women in the basement. Glasgow was probably an hour away and sending Daniel there might have given her time to release the women in the cellar, but what if he took the keys? Then she'd use the tools from the garage or she'd run until she found help. 'Would you mind? Tell them I'm safe. That I'll be back soon.'

'Of course. I'll head over this evening. If you're sure you'll be okay.' His eyes appeared soft and kind, but she knew better than to trust him.

'What day is it?' she asked.

'Saturday.'

'There's plenty of shows I can watch on telly. I'll be fine alone for a couple of hours.'

He frowned and Amalthea hoped he didn't suspect anything. He walked across to the coffee pot and she noticed him glance towards the keys hanging beside the back door. She prayed she'd replaced them exactly as they were and they weren't moving in a way that suggested they'd been recently touched.

'Tell me about yourself,' Amalthea said as he passed her a mug.

His eyes lit up and a huge smile washed over his face. 'Really?'

'Yes. If we're going to be living here together for a while maybe I'll write about you as one of my characters. Would you like that?' she asked.

He nodded.

So he is vain. I can use that. 'Where were you born?'

He sat down at the table. 'In a town called Cirencester. Have you heard of it?'

She shook her head.

'It's a small town in the West of England. Pretty, I guess. I lived on the outskirts, between the town and some woods. How about you?'

'Me?' She wasn't expecting the question to be asked in return and felt on edge. *I bet you know all about me.*

'Where were you born?'

She shrugged, dismissively. 'Oh, in Glasgow, on a rather ugly high-rise estate. Do you have any brothers or sisters?'

'I have two half-sisters. We don't really see much of each other though. You?'

'I'm an only child. After my dad left, Mum wasn't really interested in dating. She thought all men were bastards.' Amalthea laughed, nervously.

'I suspect you've inherited a little of that.' Daniel smiled.

Amalthea shrugged. 'Probably.'

'Have you ever had a boyfriend?' he asked.

'Once, about four years ago. It lasted a week. How about you?'

'No boyfriends,' he laughed. 'A fair few girlfriends, but nothing that's really lasted.'

'Are you rich?'

He narrowed his eyes and shifted uncomfortably in his seat. 'Yeah, I guess so, but I've never really thought about it.'

'I'm not. I struggle to get by. I hope I still have my job when I get back though. Speak to my boss, please. I can't afford to lose it.'

'Sure. How long have you been working there?' Daniel asked.

'About a year,' she answered, vaguely.

'I'm sure they won't sack you.'

Amalthea frowned. 'Bar work… it ties in with Uni or College. They'll replace me really quickly if I don't show.'

'I'll make sure I give him a good reason for your short absence,' he promised.

'How short?' Amalthea's tongue flicked out to moisten her lips.

Daniel seemed to relax. 'I guess that depends.'

~ 9 ~

After a light supper of grilled aubergine bake, the left overs of which were enough to feed at least four more people, Amalthea made her excuses and vacated the kitchen, saying she needed a bath. Daniel told her he'd wait until she came back down then head off to Glasgow to speak to her boss and check on her friends. She thanked him.

She put her ear to the bathroom floor, hoping to hear Daniel's movements below, but any sounds were silenced by the distance between them, so she gave up and ran a bath, pouring scented oil into the water and humming in what she hoped was a natural and relaxed way. She wanted to put him at ease so he wouldn't decide to stay.

When she returned to the kitchen the plates had been washed and the left overs were gone. He checked again that she was comfortable with his leaving. She said yes and headed for the living room to switch on the television.

'You really watch this stuff?' he asked.

'Never miss an episode.' She exhaled audibly and coughed to cover it up, silently cursing her nervousness. 'It's a window into people's lives, like watching people argue in the club.'

He frowned but didn't ask more. She was relieved. Part of her wanted to blurt out that she was lying and beg his forgiveness, but she held that part firmly in check. *Go, go, go,* she pleaded silently.

'Okay then.' He checked his watch. 'I imagine it'll take me at least three hours to get everything done, so expect me back at around ten or a bit later. Do you need anything while I'm out?'

'Have we got enough coffee?'

He grinned. 'I'll buy some more.'

He jangled his keys and left the room, heading towards the garage. She listened for the car engine and within five minutes heard it pull away from the house. She switched off the television set and peered through the window to make certain he'd gone. She stood behind the curtain for at least five minutes, terrified he had forgotten something and would return, or that his absence was a trick, a test, and he would walk back up the driveway at any moment. As time ticked away, she balanced the risk of delaying too long or not long enough and decided just standing there was making her feel sick. She withdrew from the window and left the room.

The keys were no longer on the hook. She tried the cellar door – locked. She hurried to the garage and found a crowbar and powerful shears that she hoped might tackle a metal chain. She took a saw as well in case the shears weren't strong or sharp enough. Juggling everything, afraid of dropping something sharp and heavy on her feet, she made her way back to the kitchen.

The gap between door and jam was just wide enough for the tip of the crowbar. She pushed it into the gap and strained against the handle. The door wobbled and a chunk of wood splintered off. Amalthea's heart beat faster. There was no turning back now. She would have to flee when this was done. Where would they go?

She decided not to think about that just yet. *Get the door open first, think about other things later.*

She forced the crowbar into the gap and pushed down on the handle. With a satisfyingly loud click, the door swung open towards her. Leaving the crowbar on the top stair she reached for the light pull. Cold light illuminated the room and, absolutely terrified, she proceeded, feeling as though she was descending into hell itself, dreading what she might find beyond that archway.

'Hello,' she called out.

'You're back,' a rasping voice replied.

She braced herself for whatever she might find, and entered a smaller room. On a mattress at the far side a naked woman was curled up and appeared to be unconscious, perhaps sleeping. Beside her was a plate full of the same bake she and Daniel had eaten for dinner and a plastic beaker full of red liquid.

'Over here,' the voice called.

Amalthea stepped through another archway into a similarly sized alcove and saw a second woman; this one was sitting up and her green eyes blinked rapidly as if the light hurt them. Around her throat was a metal collar with a chain that was attached to the wall.

'Next room,' the voice summoned Amalthea.

'Just a moment,' she answered and knelt down in front of the woman. The smell hurt her nose and she realised the mattress was probably drenched in urine. The woman had angry sores on her legs and stomach and was dressed in a tiny negligée that was split at the front and revealed almost all of her desperately thin body. Her ash blonde hair was long and tangled and Amalthea wondered how long she had been Daniel's prisoner. Was this what would become of Amalthea if he returned too quickly?

'That's Charlie,' the voice said.

'How long have you been here?' Amalthea asked.

The blonde woman didn't answer.

'She likes music. Switch the radio on.'

Amalthea spotted a small music player. She turned it on and music filled the space. It was risky; she wouldn't be able to hear if Daniel approached, however the joy on Charlie's face made it worthwhile. The emaciated woman seemed transported by the sound, away from this dank and filthy dungeon to somewhere beautiful. Amalthea crossed the threshold to yet another room.

In front of Amalthea there stood a pale-skinned, dark-haired beauty, completely naked except for a piece of black cloth that was wrapped around her eyes. Her body was thin, but she appeared stronger than the others.

'Hello, I'm Tay.'

The woman fumbled with the knot in her blindfold.

'Can I help?' Amalthea asked.

She fiercely shook her head. 'I can do it.'

Finally the delicate fingers succeeded in untying the knot, and she removed the cloth from her eyes. 'I'm Moira.' She blinked rapidly, opening and closing her pale blue eyes against the bright light.

Amalthea showed her the shears and handsaw. 'One of these has got to break the chains, right?'

'Are you setting us free?' the woman asked.

'Yes,' Amalthea answered.

'That's what I should have done.' Tears rolled down Moira's face.

Amalthea stepped forward and embraced her. Moira smelled repugnant and trembled violently within Amalthea's grasp, but Amalthea did not pull away for a long time, not until the woman managed to compose herself.

'May I?' Moira asked, extending a hand towards Amalthea.

Amalthea nodded and passed across the heavy cutters. The sudden weight dragged on Moria's arm, but she recovered herself quickly. She sat on the floor with her legs spread as she lined up the chain in front of her and held it in place under her knees then lifted the middle section a little and placed it within the gaping mouth of the shears. Using both her hands, making her biceps tremble, she pushed the mouth closed and with a loud snap, followed by two clunks, the chain was severed. Moira leapt up and rushed to the next bed to release Charlie.

The three of them continued to the sleeping woman.

'Diane,' Moira said, shaking her arm gently.

The woman's eyes flicked open; they were a strange violet hue that seemed to clash with her mousey-brown hair.

'This is Tay. She's setting us free.'

'Free?' Diane asked. She pushed herself up to a seated position and held the chain out for all to see.

Moira grabbed hold and snapped it as easily as she had broken the others.

'Can you walk?' Moira asked.

Diane stood up. 'I think so.'

Moira faced Amalthea and clasped both her hands. 'Before we leave this place there is something I must do. Will you help us again?'

Amalthea nodded. 'What is it?'

'We have to kill him.'

Amalthea gasped. 'Daniel?'

'Is that going to be a problem for you?' Moira asked.

Amalthea stared into Moira's defiant eyes and felt completely humbled by the power of this captured beauty. 'How?'

'Did you notice any weapons around the place?'

'There's a sword above the fireplace. I don't know if it's sharp,' Amalthea said.

'Okay, we'll test it.' Moira cut the chain again and picked up a five foot segment of it. 'This will keep him at bay for a while. You three can have a chain each. I'm taking the sword.'

'What are you going to do?' Amalthea asked.

'We're going to wait for him to come home and I will sever his head from his body.'

Amalthea gasped. 'Do you think you can?'

'I fucking know I can, Tay. I've never felt so strong in all my life,' Moira said.

Amalthea considered the two other women. It was obvious they did not share Moira's strength. 'Maybe we should get them to safety first?'

'They won't be able to walk far. How far are we from the nearest town?'

'A long way, I think,' Amalthea answered.

'We'll need his car.'

'He's taken it with him.'

'When will he be back?' Moira asked.

Amalthea checked her watch. 'Might be as little as an hour, but more likely two.'

'Okay. We'll get washed and I'm afraid we'll need to borrow some clothes.' Moira used a hand flourish to demonstrate her nakedness while Amalthea focused on the woman's face. 'And we need to figure out the best place to wait for him.'

'The workshop,' Amalthea said.

'Where?' Moira asked, eagerly.

'I'll show you. He needs to go through it to get from the garage to the house. We can wait behind the door.'

'What if he smells us?' Diane asked.

Moira and Amalthea looked at Diane simultaneously as if they had both forgotten they were not completely alone.

'If we get really clean perhaps he won't. Whatever happens though, we need to do this. We need to stop that bastard,' Moira said through gritted teeth. 'If we don't – even if we somehow manage to hide from him for the rest of our lives – there will be more victims. He's sick and he isn't going to stop. Not unless we stop him.'

'I'm afraid,' Diane admitted.

Charlie nodded in agreement.

'Of course you are,' Moira said. Her eyes were soft and gentle but her words were cold and hard. 'I am too.'

'They can wait in my room,' Amalthea suggested.

'So he can find them if we fail?' Moira said. 'This might be our only chance to go home. We should do this together.'

'I know he's a man, but with four against one the odds are absolutely in our favour. He can't be that strong.' Amalthea looked at each woman in turn and exuded the strength she knew they needed to see.

'She doesn't know,' Diane said.

Amalthea looked from Diane to Moira. 'Know what?'

Charlie fell to the floor; the movement was dramatic yet strangely graceful. She bent her throat and pointed to her jugular vein.

Amalthea shrugged. 'I don't understand.'

'Daniel is a vampire,' Moira said.

Amalthea laughed then covered her mouth and stood silently. She had no words with which to answer. The three women's faces told her that they believed what they were saying and she imagined how frightened he must have made them, day after day. It was no wonder that they had made the man into a monster in their collective imaginations. He was a monster, albeit not one with supernatural powers.

~ 10 ~

Diane and Charlie slouched on a sofa.

'You two should get washed up,' Moira said as she lifted the ornate sword off two hooks above the fireplace. 'Tay, would you help them get organised?'

Amalthea nodded, although really she wanted to watch Moira handle the katana. Moira stroked the enamelled sheath with her left hand as she held the handle in her right then she grasped the case and pulled the sword free. The steel glinted cruelly. It certainly appeared sharp enough.

'Please, Tay, we need you.'

The plea broke through Amalthea's reverie and she took the women to the upstairs bathroom. She ran a warm but not too hot bath. She reached for a bottle of oil, but decided against pouring it into the water. *Even a pleasant smell might give them away*. She helped Charlie out of her negligee and supported each woman as they climbed into the bath. Their hair was filthy and tangled and Amalthea washed it for them. Both the women looked much better without the grime.

'Dry yourselves,' she told them. 'I'll be back in a moment.'

She rushed down the stairs and came face to face with Moira who was standing, sword in hand, with a wide grin on her face.

'It's sharp.' Moira pointed at a chair in the far corner of the room or more accurately an ex-chair that had been sliced in two. One half leaned against a wall and the other rocked on its jagged side on the floor.

'Wow!' Amalthea nodded.

'I'd better get cleaned up. Can we borrow some clothes?'

'Of course. Follow me.'

Amalthea jogged up the stairs as Moira followed behind with the unsheathed sword still in her hand.

'Be careful with that,' Amalthea said.

'Uhh, oh yeah.' Moira chuckled.

Amalthea waited at the top of the stairs for the unlikely warriors to return, unable to stop her body from shaking, terrified of what was to come. Amalthea wasn't sure she wanted Daniel to die. He was a monster, but surely running away and letting the authorities deal with him was the only solution that made sense in a civilised world, certainly not slicing someone into pieces. There were too many things that could go wrong with Moira's plan. What if they froze, unable strike the fatal blow? What would he do then? She stared at the bathroom door, trying to find words to convince Moira of the folly of her plan. *What if it were me, chained up in the basement? Would I want to kill him?* At least this way the women would have closure of one kind or another.

The three women stepped out from the bathroom. Amalthea's clothes fit them poorly, but even so it was wonderful to see them looking... human. No longer chained animals or slaves, but people who were able to make their own choices, their own mistakes. Amalthea's fear subsided as she realised she wasn't responsible for them. It was time to let them make their own decisions, and if that meant killing Daniel, so be it. She would not stand in their way and, if needed, she would help them.

Moira held the sword confidently and the smile on her face was beautiful and calm, empowered.

'Show us this workshop, please Tay,' Moira said.

'Is this what you all want to do?' Amalthea asked.

All three nodded.

'It's what we have to do,' Moira answered.

Amalthea led the way. Moira checked the door to the garage and found that it opened towards them into the workshop, creating a blind spot that would fit one person easily, two at a squeeze.

She peered into the garage. Amalthea flicked on the light and a fluorescent strip blinked into life.

'Nowhere in there. I guess we'll all have to wait in here. So how are we going to do this? The door will open and block this area from Daniel's vision. Diane and Charlie do you want to stand behind there with the chains? I can wait on the other side. If he sees me before I get chance to swing I'll need you to restrain him as best you can with those chains, okay?'

'Where do you want me?' Amalthea asked.

Moira smiled in a way that sent shivers of anticipation along Amalthea's spine. 'How about in that corner?' She pointed at the far left wall, facing the garage door. 'Do you want a chain or the crowbar?'

'Crowbar,' Amalthea answered.

'Good choice.' Moira winked.

Amalthea blushed. Like a teenager crushing on an older girl at school, she was as much in love with Moira's poise and commanding personality as she was with her beauty. She desperately hoped that, when all this was over, she'd have the chance to get to know the woman better.

'Light on or light off?' Amalthea asked.

'Off,' the three said together.

'But will we be able to see well enough to attack?' Amalthea asked.

'We've been living in a dark cellar for months. We can see in the dark. Plus chances are the garage will be lit. Did you switch the light off in there?'

Amalthea opened the garage door and switched off the light.

'Ready?' Moira asked.

The women got into position and Moira extinguished the light. Only a tiny sliver of illumination, from the hallway beyond, remained.

'Maybe we should sit while we wait?' Amalthea said.

'Don't fall asleep,' Moira warned.

'I don't think we'll have time. Unless I'm mistaken, isn't that the sound of a car engine?' Amalthea whispered.

'I can hear it too,' Moira said. 'Okay, stand up, it's show time.'

~ 11 ~

The garage door chugged upwards and the clanking of chains made the room feel colder. Amalthea imagined the others were shivering with dread too – he had returned. *What now?* She opened her mouth to renegotiate on Daniel's behalf or was it on her behalf, but swallowed the words. He didn't deserve their mercy. *Chaining Moira for all those months, years... How dare one imprison such a wild spirit?* It was unforgivable, and Amalthea would not plead for his life, but what if they failed? What if the women crumpled and folded as he stepped into the room? Would it be up to Amalthea to finish what Moira started? She didn't know whether she could. The word *wait* rose to her throat like a hiccup, but at that moment the car engine was switched off and the rooms descended into a silence that was broken only by the squeak of a car door opening and the sound of suction as it was pushed closed, the tapping of footsteps and the churning and clunking of chains as the garage door descended. There was no light beyond the door. Daniel did what he needed to do in the dark and Amalthea suddenly realised that he would see them the moment he stepped into the room. Her fear rose to a new precipice and she smelled panic around her as the same realisation dawned on the others, but it was too late to run. Amalthea raised the crowbar and made ready to strike – strike then run – if she knocked him out, they might still get away alive.

She heard the door handle click then silence returned. She imagined him waiting on the other side of that narrow wood barrier, knowing their exact positions in the workshop. He knew they were waiting in the dark for his return and that Amalthea had betrayed him, rescuing and releasing the women he had chained in the dark. She sensed his anger and bitter disappointment as he paced around the garage, deciding what to do. She checked her imagination; he wasn't pacing the length of the garage; there was no sound of footsteps. For some reason, that Amalthea was unable to fathom, he was standing perfectly still behind the door. What was he waiting for?

Time crawled as if someone pressed a button marked slow motion. Every breath Amalthea took seemed to last an hour, and she focused on the progression of air into and out of her lungs millimetre by agonising millimetre. The time between exhaling and inhaling made her panic as if she would run out of air and die. The taunting cruelty of her own imagination caused her to visualise the fine hairs on Daniel's hand, in the darkness; she watched a bead of sweat blossom and roll down his brow. He didn't move his hand to wipe it away and his fingers lingered, motionless, less than an inch from the door handle, caught in a bubble of time that seemed as though it would last an eternity then the door clicked and time sped up. Before Amalthea realised what was happening Daniel stood in the workshop surrounded by the three women. She watched helplessly as Diane and Charlie wrapped chains around his wrists. He shook his right arm and Diane flew against a wall and bounced off it onto the floor. Moira held the sword in two hands behind her shoulder and swung. He ducked and it whistled through the air above his head. Taking a step back, Moira reversed the sword and swung again.

'Daniel,' Amalthea said.

He faced her. Tears rolled down his cheeks and his eyes pleaded for an answer to one question. "Why?"

'You can't make prisoners out of people,' Amalthea said, although she wasn't entirely sure whether she made any noise at all; perhaps she just thought the answer.

'I only wanted…'

With an elegant yet ruthless swing, the sword hit Daniel's neck on its second arc and cut into his spinal cord. Moira tugged it away from the bone and muscle, and Daniel's head hung at an odd angle, but he kept speaking. 'To be…'

A slash from the opposite side hacked into his throat. The skin flapped open and the muscle beneath created a grotesque necklace.

'Loved.'

With a final, full-body swing, so powerful it made Moira stagger and lose her footing, Daniel's head was severed. It flew through the air towards Amalthea, landing dramatically at her feet. His eyes stared up at her. The bloodless, bodyless head stared into her eyes, mouth still moving, dimpled cheeks still twitching. Amalthea had fallen down the rabbit hole; it wasn't happening. It wasn't real. *Wake up!*

'I'm sorry.' His last words were spoken and his face was no longer animated; Amalthea released the scream she'd been holding and the sound echoed around the workshop. The other women covered their ears to protect themselves from the relentlessly slicing sound.

She sensed a presence beside her and two shaking arms were wrapped around her upper body. She stopped screaming.

'It's time to go,' Moira said.

'What just happened?' Amalthea asked trying to drag air into her empty lungs.

'He's dead,' Moira answered. 'Let's go.'

Amalthea shook her head, but Moira clasped her hand and pulled her towards the garage. As they passed Daniel's headless body, Charlie knelt beside it searching his pockets. She pulled out and jangled a set of keys.

'Should we bury him?' Diane asked.

'I just want to go home,' Moira said.

Amalthea heard the conversation and tried to nod, but she felt as distant as a star and completely unable to communicate.

'We'll go to Glasgow first. Hopefully we can get some sense out of her when we hit the city.'

Moira pushed Amalthea into the front passenger seat and strapped a seat belt around her torso. Diane and Charlie got into the back as Moira fired up the engine and switched on the lights. 'Dammit. The doors.'

'I'll get them,' Charlie said, bounding excitedly out of the car like a puppy on its first walk.

Amalthea stared blankly as the metal door shunted upwards. Moira drove beneath it to their freedom.

'There was no blood,' Amalthea whispered.

'Welcome back, Tay. I thought we lost you back there. What did you say?' Moira asked.

They were still in the car. Amalthea peered at the other two cuddled and asleep on the back seat. Moira seemed alert and comfortable driving.

'No blood,' Amalthea repeated, finding her voice.

'I guess that's what happens with vampires.' Moira shrugged.

'Vampires don't exist,' Amalthea said.

'Then you explain why his neck didn't bleed when we chopped off his head?'

'I can't.'

'Vampire,' Moira said, firmly.

Amalthea nodded. She had no better answer. 'How did you know?'

'That he wasn't human?'

'Yes.'

'A thousand little things and a few larger ones: he barely touched any food and when he did it seemed like he was just trying to appear normal. He stank of blood; I saw dried remains of it in the crease of his mouth once or twice. He even told me when I asked. I was chained up by then, of course, but I knew he was telling me the truth at last,' Moira said.

'I didn't know. I thought you were just scared of him.' Hot tears formed in Amalthea's eyes.

'Vampires exist.'

'You don't think he's the only one?' Amalthea asked.

'He may be a freak, but he never struck me as something marvellously unique.'

~ 12 ~

'What about a world trip?' Amalthea asked, resting her head on Moira's shoulder.

Five months had passed. Amalthea had been busy, and now she was living in the tiny Camden bedsit with the love of her life. Writing about vampires, researching them, had become an obsession, but she had no idea what was true and what was fiction.

'The writing might make you a target.' Moira squeezed Amalthea's hand and kissed her fingers.

'Babes, we're already targets. We killed one of them. You think I should stop?'

Moira shrugged then shook her head, stopped and shrugged again. 'I don't know. Sometimes I get scared. It feels like we're being watched.'

Amalthea glanced involuntarily at the window with its closed blind and drawn curtains – belt and braces. 'If they thought we were a threat they'd have already dealt with us.'

'I guess so. I just don't want to lose you. I don't think being so open about what we're doing is the way to go.'

'But it's how we found Robert,' Amalthea said.

'Robert's crazy,' Moira replied.

Amalthea sighed.

'You want danger?' Moira asked.

'I don't know. I want something I can sink my teeth into if you'll excuse the pun.'

Moira grinned and stroked Amalthea's wrist. 'You can sink your teeth into me.'

'Mmmmm.' Amalthea nibbled Moira's throat.

Moira arched her neck and exposed her fluttering pulse for further oral investigation. They kissed and the world spun around them. Hands explored each other's bodies.

Moira pushed Amalthea off her body. 'I just wonder…'

'What?'

Moira stared hard into Amalthea's eyes. 'Whether we're better off letting it go.'

'Always wondering who's waiting round the next corner?' Amalthea asked.

'You sound paranoid,' Moira said.

'Daniel can't be the only one. You said it yourself. There might be hundreds of vampires out there. We don't know. We'll probably never know.'

Moira glanced up at the two katana swords that hung on their apartment wall, more than a simple decoration. 'I wonder what they are?'

'Vampires?'

'Yes. Did Stoker get it right? Are they cursed or are they something else? A genetic mutation or a different species?' Moira pondered.

Amalthea tucked a stray hair behind her ear. 'Does it matter?'

Moira nodded. 'I think so. Know your enemy.'

'Understand your characters.'

'So, what do you want to do this evening? Are we gonna fuck or what?' Moira asked.

Amalthea kissed Moira's hand. 'Yes.'

Amalthea and Moira's Lesbian Vampire-Slaying adventures will continue in 2022 with "Penthouse Beauties" by Carmilla Voiez.

www.carmillavoiez.com

Discover Carmilla's full bibliography at http://smarturl.it/CarmillaOnAmazon.